SNOWBOARDING

By Meg Gaertner

WWW.APEXEDITIONS.COM

Copyright © 2022 by Apex Editions, Mendota Heights, MN 55120. All rights reserved. No part of this book may be reproduced or utilized in any form or by any means without written permission from the publisher.

Apex is distributed by North Star Editions:
sales@northstareditions.com | 888-417-0195

Produced for Apex by Red Line Editorial.

Photographs ©: Gregory Bull/AP Images, cover, 1; Shutterstock Images, 4–5, 6, 9, 12, 13, 14, 15, 16–17, 18, 19, 20, 21, 22–23, 24, 25, 26–27, 29; iStockphoto, 7; Chris Dillmann/Vail Daily/AP Images, 8; jackrcoyne/Stockimo/Alamy, 10–11

Library of Congress Control Number: 2021915736

ISBN
978-1-63738-155-7 (hardcover)
978-1-63738-191-5 (paperback)
978-1-63738-261-5 (ebook pdf)
978-1-63738-227-1 (hosted ebook)

Printed in the United States of America
Mankato, MN
012022

NOTE TO PARENTS AND EDUCATORS

Apex books are designed to build literacy skills in striving readers. Exciting, high-interest content attracts and holds readers' attention. The text is carefully leveled to allow students to achieve success quickly. Additional features, such as bolded glossary words for difficult terms, help build comprehension.

TABLE OF CONTENTS

CHAPTER 1
INTO THE HALF-PIPE 5

CHAPTER 2
HISTORY OF THE SPORT 11

CHAPTER 3
SNOWBOARDING EVENTS 17

CHAPTER 4
PREPARING TO RIDE 23

Comprehension Questions • 28
Glossary • 30
To Learn More • 31
About the Author • 31
Index • 32

CHAPTER 1

INTO THE HALF-PIPE

The rider flies down a snowy hill. She enters a **half-pipe** made of packed snow.

Snowboarders go one at a time in a half-pipe event.

The rider zooms down one wall of the half-pipe. She shoots up the other wall. She soars into the air and does a trick.

Half-pipes can be between 11 and 22 feet (3–7 m) high.

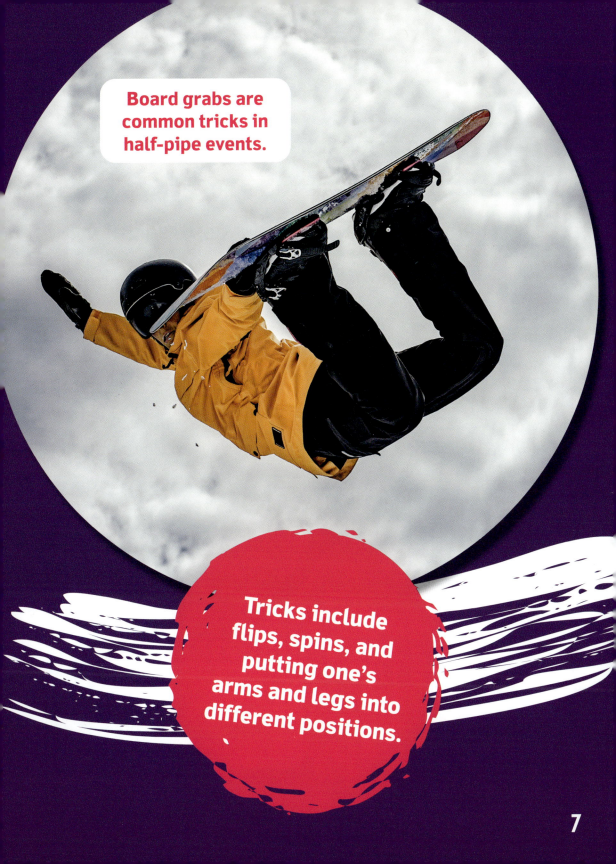

Board grabs are common tricks in half-pipe events.

Tricks include flips, spins, and putting one's arms and legs into different positions.

7

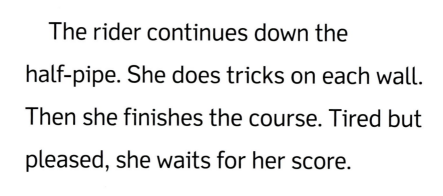

The rider continues down the half-pipe. She does tricks on each wall. Then she finishes the course. Tired but pleased, she waits for her score.

Half-pipe scores are based on how difficult the tricks are and how well riders do them.

Chloe Kim celebrates after winning an Olympic gold medal in 2018.

YOUNG SUPERSTAR

Chloe Kim won gold in the 2018 Olympic half-pipe event. She was only 17 years old. She was the youngest woman to win Olympic snowboarding gold.

CHAPTER 2
HISTORY OF THE SPORT

In 1965, a man stuck two skis together. He rode them down the hill in his backyard. Then he began selling his early snowboard.

The first type of snowboard was called the Snurfer. The name is a mix of *snow* and *surfer*.

In the 1970s, people modified the board. They added straps for the rider's feet. They also gave the board's surface greater **traction**.

Straps keep a rider's boots in place on the snowboard.

Today, many people ski and snowboard at resorts.

At first, ski resorts wouldn't allow snowboarding on their slopes. Snowboarders would sneak in at night to ride downhill.

The first national competition was in 1982. Snowboarding grew in popularity. In 1998, it became a Winter Olympics event.

Snowboarding was the fastest-growing winter sport in the 1990s.

Early competitions were races only. Then they expanded to trick-based events.

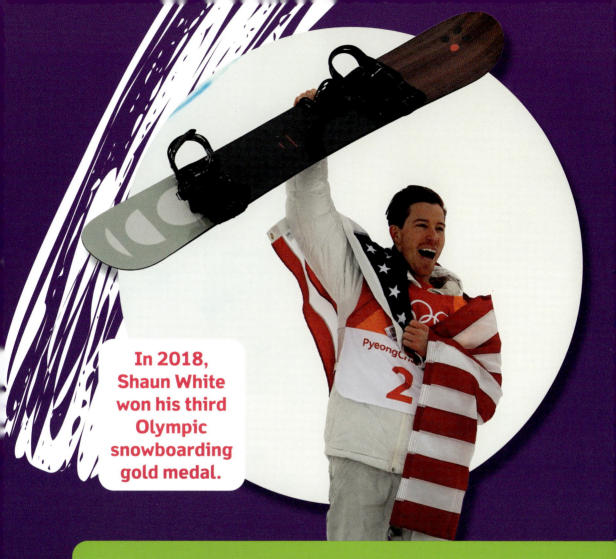

In 2018, Shaun White won his third Olympic snowboarding gold medal.

SNOWBOARDING LEGEND

Shaun White won gold at the 2006 Winter Olympics. In 2005–06, he had a perfect season. He won all 12 of his competitions.

CHAPTER 3

SNOWBOARDING EVENTS

Some snowboarding events are races. The fastest riders move to the next round. Once only 16 riders are left, they race **head-to-head**.

In parallel giant slalom, riders race in pairs.

Other events involve tricks. In slopestyle, riders zoom down an **obstacle course**. They slide down rails. They fly off jumps and up **quarter-pipes**. They do tricks in midair.

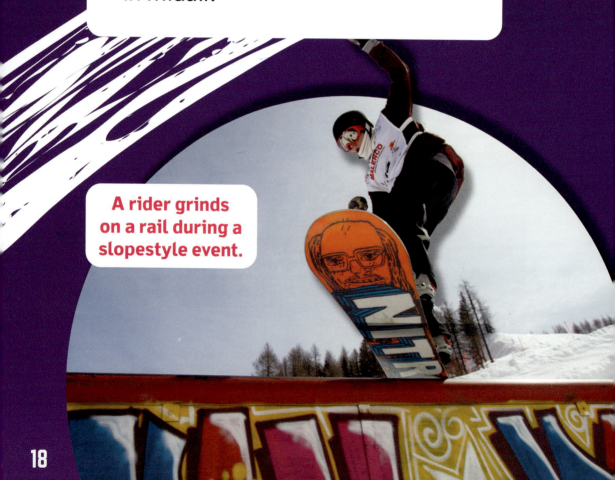

A rider grinds on a rail during a slopestyle event.

In a handplant, a rider grabs the top of a quarter-pipe. Then he or she sticks the snowboard out.

In 2007, a snowboarder set a record for highest air. He went 32 feet (10 m) above the top of a quarter-pipe.

Flips can get riders lots of points in competitions.

Riders grab their boards. They do flips. They spin forward or backward. Some even spin multiple times in one jump.

THE FIRST 1980

Spin tricks are named for how much riders turn in the air. In 2017, Yuki Kadono did the world's first 1980. This means he spun five and a half times in midair.

In big air, riders take off on a very large jump. They do a huge trick. Then they land.

CHAPTER 4
PREPARING TO RIDE

Snowboards come in a variety of lengths, widths, and shapes. Different boards work best on different **terrains**.

Speed riders tend to use longer boards. Trick riders often use shorter boards that are easier to turn.

All-mountain boards work well on any terrain. Powder boards are for riding on deep snow. Freeride boards are used on **ungroomed** slopes. Light freestyle boards are for doing tricks.

Freeride boards are good for riding out in nature. They can handle lots of kinds of snow.

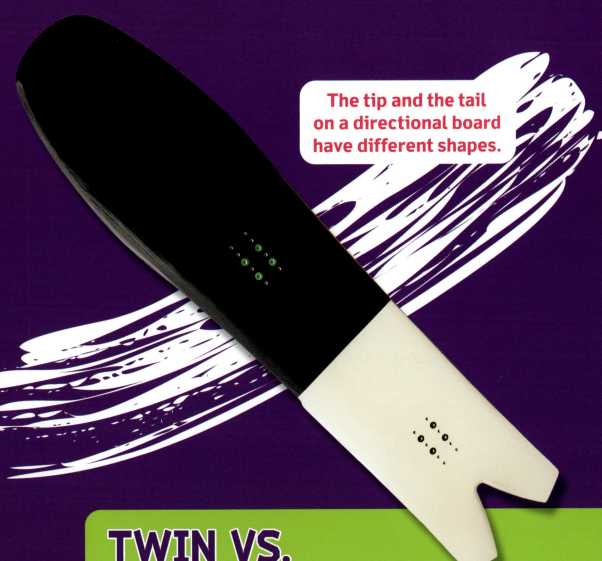

The tip and the tail on a directional board have different shapes.

TWIN VS. DIRECTIONAL

Twin boards can be ridden with either end forward. Directional boards are meant to be ridden just one way. One end always points down the hill.

Riders wear layers for warmth. They wear waterproof jackets and pants. They use helmets for head protection. Strong boots prevent foot and ankle pain.

Goggles and sunscreen help with snow glare.

Snowboard gear helps riders stay safe in the snow, wind, and cold.

COMPREHENSION QUESTIONS

Write your answers on a separate piece of paper.

1. Write a paragraph summarizing the different snowboarding events.

2. Which snowboarding event would you most want to see? Why?

3. How old was Chloe Kim when she won her first Olympic gold medal?

    A. 14

    B. 17

    C. 20

4. Why might it be hard to do a trick like a 1980?

    A. Riders need to jump very high to spin that many times.

    B. Riders need to go extra slow to spin that many times.

    C. Riders need to go upside down to spin that many times.

5. What does **modified** mean in this book?

*In the 1970s, people **modified** the board. They added straps for the rider's feet.*

    A. made changes
    B. rode downhill
    C. sold in stores

6. What does **variety** mean in this book?

*Snowboards come in a **variety** of lengths, widths, and shapes. Different boards work best on different terrains.*

    A. having no shape
    B. having all the same type
    C. having many different types

Answer key on page 32.

GLOSSARY

half-pipe
A U-shaped course that snowboarders go back and forth across.

head-to-head
Competing at the same time on the same course.

obstacle course
A path filled with things that block the rider's way.

quarter-pipes
Half of half-pipes. Each quarter-pipe is a single curved slope.

resorts
Places where people on vacation can stay and have fun doing various activities.

snow glare
Sunlight that bounces off the snow and into a rider's eyes and face.

terrains
Areas of land with different features.

traction
Grip that helps a rider's boots stick to the snowboard and remain stable.

ungroomed
Not smoothed over or made ready for snowboarding.

TO LEARN MORE

BOOKS

Abdo, Kenny. *Snowboarding*. Minneapolis: Abdo Publishing, 2018.

Chandler, Matt. *Chloe Kim: Gold-Medal Snowboarder*. North Mankato, MN: Capstone Press, 2020.

Kenney, Karen Latchana. *Extreme Snowboarding Challenges*. Minneapolis: Lerner Publications, 2021.

ONLINE RESOURCES

Visit **www.apexeditions.com** to find links and resources related to this title.

ABOUT THE AUTHOR

Meg Gaertner is a children's book editor and writer. She lives in Minneapolis, where she enjoys swing dancing and spending time outside.

INDEX

A
all-mountain boards, 24

D
directional boards, 25

F
flips, 7, 20
freeride boards, 24

H
half-pipes, 5–6, 8–9
helmets, 26

K
Kadono, Yuki, 21
Kim, Chloe, 9

L
light freestyle boards, 24

O
Olympics, 9, 14–15

P
powder boards, 24

Q
quarter-pipes, 18–19

R
races, 17
resorts, 13

S
slopestyle, 18
spins, 7, 20–21

T
tricks, 6–8, 18, 21, 24
twin boards, 25

W
White, Shaun, 15

Answer Key:
1. Answers will vary; **2.** Answers will vary; **3.** B; **4.** A; **5.** A; **6.** C